Thomas Bailey Aldrich

Unguarded Gates

And other Poems

Thomas Bailey Aldrich

Unguarded Gates
And other Poems

ISBN/EAN: 9783744770187

Printed in Europe, USA, Canada, Australia, Japan

Cover: Foto ©Andreas Hilbeck / pixelio.de

More available books at **www.hansebooks.com**

UNGUARDED GATES

AND OTHER POEMS

BY

THOMAS BAILEY ALDRICH

BOSTON AND NEW YORK
HOUGHTON, MIFFLIN AND COMPANY
The Riverside Press, Cambridge
1895

The Riverside Press, Cambridge, Mass., U. S. A.
Electrotyped and Printed by H. O. Houghton & Co.

CONTENTS

	PAGE
PRELUDE	7
UNGUARDED GATES	13
ELMWOOD	18
A SHADOW OF THE NIGHT	25
SEA LONGINGS	28
THE LAMENT OF EL MOULOK	31
NECROMANCY	34
WHITE EDITH	35
INTERLUDES —	
Insomnia	49
Seeming Defeat	52
Two Moods	54
A Parable	57
"Great Captain, glorious in our Wars"	58
A Refrain	60
At Nijnii-Novgorod	61
The Winter Robin	64
The Sailing of the Autocrat	65
Cradle Song	68
Broken Music	69
Art	72

INTERLUDES—

    "When from the tense chords of that mighty lyre" 74

    A Serenade 76

    A Bridal Measure 78

    Imogen 80

SEVEN SONNETS—

    Outward Bound 85

    Ellen Terry in "The Merchant of Venice" . . 87

    The Poets 89

    The Undiscovered Country 91

    Books and Seasons 93

    Reminiscence 95

    Andromeda 97

NOURMADEE 99

FOOTNOTES—

    Fireflies 117

    Problem 117

    Originality 118

    Kismet 118

    A Hint from Herrick 119

    Pessimistic Poets 119

    Hospitality 120

    Points of View 120

    The Two Masks 121

    Quits 121

PRELUDE

PRELUDE

In youth, beside the lonely sea,

Voices and visions came to me.

Titania and her furtive broods

Were my familiars in the woods.

From every flower that broke in flame,

Some half-articulate whisper came.

In every wind I felt the stir

Of some celestial messenger.

Later, amid the city's din
And toil and wealth and want and sin,

They followed me from street to street,
The dreams that made my boyhood sweet.

As in the silence-haunted glen,
So, mid the crowded ways of men,

Strange lights my errant fancy led,
Strange watchers watched beside my bed.

Ill fortune had no shafts for me
In this aerial company.

Now one by one the visions fly,
And one by one the voices die.

More distantly the accents ring,

More frequent the receding wing.

Full dark shall be the days in store,

When voice and vision come no more !

UNGUARDED GATES

UNGUARDED GATES

WIDE open and unguarded stand our gates,

Named of the four winds, North, South, East, and

West ;

Portals that lead to an enchanted land

Of cities, forests, fields of living gold,

Vast prairies, lordly summits touched with snow,

Majestic rivers sweeping proudly past

The Arab's date-palm and the Norseman's

pine —

A realm wherein are fruits of every zone,

Airs of all climes, for lo ! throughout the year

The red rose blossoms somewhere — a rich land,

A later Eden planted in the wilds,

With not an inch of earth within its bound

But if a slave's foot press it sets him free.

Here, it is written, Toil shall have its wage,

And Honor honor, and the humblest man

Stand level with the highest in the law.

Of such a land have men in dungeons dreamed,

And with the vision brightening in their eyes

Gone smiling to the fagot and the sword.

Wide open and unguarded stand our gates,

And through them presses a wild motley throng —

Men from the Volga and the Tartar steppes,

Featureless figures of the Hoang-Ho,

Malayan, Scythian, Teuton, Kelt, and Slav,

Flying the Old World's poverty and scorn ;

These bringing with them unknown gods and rites,

Those, tiger passions, here to stretch their claws.

In street and alley what strange tongues are loud,

Accents of menace alien to our air,

Voices that once the Tower of Babel knew !

O Liberty, white Goddess ! is it well

To leave the gates unguarded ?   On thy breast

Fold Sorrow's children, soothe the hurts of fate,

Lift the down-trodden, but with hand of steel

Stay those who to thy sacred portals come

To waste the gifts of freedom.   Have a care

Lest from thy brow the clustered stars be torn

And trampled in the dust.   For so of old

The thronging Goth and Vandal trampled Rome,

And where the temples of the Cæsars stood

The lean wolf unmolested made her lair.

ELMWOOD

IN MEMORY OF JAMES RUSSELL LOWELL

HERE, in the twilight, at the well-known gate

I linger, with no heart to enter more.

Among the elm-tops the autumnal air

Murmurs, and spectral in the fading light

A solitary heron wings its way

Southward — save this no sound or touch of life.

Dark is that window where the scholar's lamp

Was used to catch a pallor from the dawn.

Yet I must needs a little linger here.

Each shrub and tree is eloquent of him,

For tongueless things and silence have their

    speech.

This is the path familiar to his foot

From infancy to manhood and old age;

For in a chamber of that ancient house

His eyes first opened on the mystery

Of life, and all the splendor of the world.

Here, as a child, in loving, curious way,

He watched the bluebird's coming; learned the

    date

Of hyacinth and goldenrod, and made

Friends of those little redmen of the elms,

And slyly added to their winter store

Of hazel-nuts : no harmless thing that breathed,

Footed or winged, but knew him for a friend.

The gilded butterfly was not afraid

To trust its gold to that so gentle hand,

The bluebird fled not from the pendent spray.

Ah, happy childhood, ringed with fortunate stars !

What dreams were his in this enchanted sphere,

What intuitions of high destiny !

The honey-bees of Hybla touched his lips

In that old New-World garden, unawares.

So in her arms did Mother Nature fold

Her poet, whispering what of wild and sweet

Into his ear — the state-affairs of birds,

The lore of dawn and sunset, what the wind

Said in the tree-tops — fine, unfathomed things

Henceforth to turn to music in his brain :

A various music, now like notes of flutes,

And now like blasts of trumpets blown in wars.

Later he paced this leafy academe

A student, drinking from Greek chalices

The ripened vintage of the antique world.

And here to him came love, and love's dear
    loss;

Here honors came, the deep applause of men

Touched to the heart by some swift-wingëd word

That from his own full heart took eager flight —

Some strain of piercing sweetness or rebuke,

For underneath his gentle nature flamed

A noble scorn for all ignoble deed,

Himself a bondman till all men were free.

Thus passed his manhood; then to other lands

He strayed, a stainless figure among courts

Beside the Manzanares and the Thames.

Whence, after too long exile, he returned

With fresher laurel, but sedater step

And eye more serious, fain to breathe the air

Where through the Cambridge marshes the blue
    Charles
Uncoils its length and stretches to the sea :
Stream dear to him, at every curve a shrine
For pilgrim Memory.   Again he watched
His loved syringa whitening by the door,
And knew the catbird's welcome ; in his walks
Smiled on his tawny kinsmen of the elms
Stealing his nuts ; and in the ruined year
Sat at his widowed hearthside with bent brows
Leonine, frosty with the breath of time,
And listened to the crooning of the wind
In the wide Elmwood chimneys, as of old.
And then — and then   .   .   .

    The after-glow has faded from the elms,
And in the denser darkness of the boughs

From time to time the firefly's tiny lamp

Sparkles.   How often in still summer dusks

He paused to note that transient phantom spark

Flash on the air — a light that outlasts him !

The night grows chill, as if it felt a breath

Blown from that frozen city where he lies.

All things turn strange.   The leaf that rustles

here

Has more than autumn's mournfulness.   The

place

Is heavy with his absence.   Like fixed eyes

Whence the dear light of sense and thought has

fled

The vacant windows stare across the lawn.

The wise sweet spirit that informed it all

Is otherwhere.   The house itself is dead.

———

O autumn wind among the sombre pines,

Breathe you his dirge, but be it sweet and low,

With deep refrains and murmurs of the sea,

Like to his verse — the art is yours alone.

His once — you taught him.   Now no voice but

    yours !

Tender and low, O wind among the pines.

I would, were mine a lyre of richer strings,

In soft Sicilian accents wrap his name.

A SHADOW OF THE NIGHT

CLOSE on the edge of a midsummer dawn

In troubled dreams I went from land to land,

Each seven-colored like the rainbow's arc,

Regions where never fancy's foot had trod

Till then ; yet all the strangeness seemed not

     strange,

At which I wondered, reasoning in my dream

With two-fold sense, well knowing that I slept.

At last I came to this our cloud-hung earth,

And somewhere by the seashore was a grave,

A woman's grave, new-made, and heaped with

     flowers ;

And near it stood an ancient holy man

That fain would comfort me, who sorrowed not

For this unknown dead woman at my feet.

But I, because his sacred office held

My reverence, listened ; and 't was thus he spake :

" When next thou comest thou shalt find her still

In all the rare perfection that she was.

Thou shalt have gentle greeting of thy love !

Her eyelids will have turned to violets,

Her bosom to white lilies, and her breath

To roses.   What is lovely never dies,

But passes into other loveliness,

Star-dust, or sea-foam, flower, or wingëd air.

If this befalls our poor unworthy flesh,

Think thee what destiny awaits the soul !

What glorious vesture it shall wear at last ! "

While yet he spoke, seashore and grave and

    priest

Vanished, and faintly from a neighboring spire

Fell five slow solemn strokes upon my ear.

Then I awoke with a keen pain at heart,

A sense of swift unutterable loss,

And through the darkness reached my hand to
touch

Her cheek, soft-pillowed on one restful palm —

To be quite sure!

SEA LONGINGS

THE first world-sound that fell upon my ear

Was that of the great winds along the coast

Crushing the deep-sea beryl on the rocks —

The distant breakers' sullen cannonade.

Against the spires and gables of the town

The white fog drifted, catching here and there

At over-leaning cornice or peaked roof,

And hung — weird gonfalons. The garden walks

Were choked with leaves, and on their ragged

    biers

Lay dead the sweets of summer — damask rose,

Clove-pink, old-fashioned, loved New England

    flowers.

Only keen salt sea-odors filled the air.

Sea-sounds, sea-odors — these were all my world.

Hence is it that life languishes with me

Inland ; the valleys stifle me with gloom

And pent-up prospect ; in their narrow bound

Imagination flutters futile wings.

Vainly I seek the sloping pearl-white sand

And the mirage's phantom citadels

Miraculous, a moment seen, then gone.

Among the mountains I am ill at ease,

Missing the stretched horizon's level line

And the illimitable restless blue.

The crag-torn sky is not the sky I love,

But one unbroken sapphire spanning all ;

And nobler than the branches of a pine

Aslant upon a precipice's edge

Are the strained spars of some great battle-ship

Plowing across the sunset.   No bird's lilt

So takes me as the whistling of the gale

Among the shrouds.   My cradle-song was this,

Strange inarticulate sorrows of the sea,

Blithe rhythms upgathered from the Sirens' caves.

Perchance of earthly voices the last voice

That shall an instant my freed spirit stay

On this world's verge, will be some message

    blown

Over the dim salt lands that fringe the coast

At dusk, or when the trancëd midnight droops

With weight of stars, or haply just as dawn,

Illumining the sullen purple wave,

Turns the gray pools and willow-stems to gold.

THE LAMENT OF EL MOULOK

WITHIN the sacred precincts of the mosque,

Even on the very steps of St. Sophia,

He lifted up his voice and spoke these words,

El Moulok, who sang naught but love-songs once,

And now was crazed because his son was dead :

O ye who leave

Your slippers at the portal, as is meet,

Give heed an instant ere ye bow in prayer.

Ages ago,

Allah, grown weary of His myriad worlds,

Would one star more to hang against the blue.

Then of men's bones,

Millions on millions, did He build the earth.

Of women's tears,

Down falling through the night, He made the sea.

Of sighs and sobs

He made the winds that surge about the globe.

Where'er ye tread,

Ye tread on dust that once was living man.

The mist and rain

Are tears that first from human eyelids fell.

The unseen winds

Breathe endless lamentation for the dead.

Not so the ancient tablets told the tale,

Not so the Koran! This was blasphemy,

And they that heard El Moulok dragged him

    hence,

Even from the very steps of St. Sophia,

And loaded him with triple chains of steel,

And cast him in a dungeon.

               None the less

Do women's tears fall ceaseless day and night,

And none the less do mortals faint and die

And turn to dust ; and every wind that blows

About the globe seems heavy with the grief

Of those who sorrow, or have sorrowed, here.

Yet none the less is Allah the Most High,

The Clement, the Compassionate. He sees

Where we are blind, and hallowed be His Name!

NECROMANCY

THROUGH a chance fissure of the churchyard
 wall
A creeping vine puts forth a single spray,
At whose slim end a starry blossom droops
Full to the soft vermilion of a rose
That reaches up on tiptoe for the kiss.
Not them the wren disturbs, nor the loud bee
That buzzes homeward with his load of sweets :
And thus they linger, flowery lip to lip,
Heedless of all, in rapturous mute embrace.
Some necromancy here ! These two, I think,
Were once unhappy lovers upon earth.

WHITE EDITH

ABOVE an ancient book, with a knight's crest

In tarnished gold on either cover stamped,

She leaned, and read — a chronicle it was

In which the sound of hautboys stirred the pulse,

And masques and gilded pageants fed the eye.

Though here and there the vellum page was
    stained

Sanguine with battle, chiefly it was love

The stylus held — some wan-cheeked scribe,
    perchance,

That in a mouldy tower by candle-light

Forgot his hunger in his madrigals.

Outside was winter : in its winding-sheet

The frozen Year lay. Silent was the room,

Save when the wind against the casement pressed

Or a page rustled, turned impatiently,

Or when along the still damp apple-wood

A little flame ran that chirped like a bird —

Some wren's ghost haunting the familiar bough.

With parted lips, in which less color lived

Than paints the pale wild-rose, she leaned and
    read.

From time to time her fingers unawares

Closed on the palm ; and oft upon her cheek

The pallor died, and left such transient glow

As might from some rich chapel window fall

On a girl's cheek at prayer. So moved her soul,

From this dull age unshackled and divorced,

In far moon-haunted gardens of romance.

But once the wind that swept the palsied oaks,

As if new-pierced with sorrow, came and moaned

Close by the casement; then she raised her eyes,

The light of dreams still fringing them, and spoke :

" Tell me, good cousin, does this book say true?

Is it so fine a thing to be a queen?"

   As if a spell of incantation dwelt

In those soft syllables, before me stood,

Colored like life, the phantasm of a maid

Who, in the savage childhood of this world,

Was crowned by error, or through dark intent

Made queen, and for the durance of one day

The royal diadem and ermine wore.

In strange sort wore — for this queen fed the starved,

The naked clothed, threw open dungeon doors ;

Could to no story list of suffering

But the full tear was lovely on her lash ;

Taught Grief to smile, and wan Despair to hope ;

Upon her stainless bosom pillowed Sin

Repentant at her feet — like Him of old ;

Made even the kerns and wild-men of the fells,

That sniffing pillage clamored at the gate,

Gentler than doves by some unknown white art,

And saying to herself, " So, I am Queen ! "

With lip all tremulous, held out her hand

To the crowd's kiss.   What joy to ease the hurt

Of bruisëd hearts !   As in a trance she walked

That live-long day.   Then night came, and the
          stars,

And blissful sleep.   But ere the birds were called

By bluebell chimes (unheard of mortal ear)

To matins in their branch-hung priories —

Ere yet the dawn its gleaming edge lay bare

Like to the burnished axe's subtle edge,

She, from her sleep's caresses roughly torn,

The meek eyes blinking in the torches' glare,

Upon a scaffold for her glory paid

Her cheeks' two roses.   For it so befell

That from the Northland there was come a prince,

With a great clash of shields and trailing spears

Through the black portals of the breathless night,

To claim the sceptre.   He no less would take

Than those same roses for his usury.

What less, in faith !   The throne was rightly his

Of that sea-girdled isle ; so to the block

Needs go the ringlets and the white swan-throat.

A touch of steel, a sudden darkness, then

Blue Heaven and all the hymning angel-choir !

No tears for her — keep tears for those who live

To mate with sin and shame, and have remorse

At last to light them to unhallowed earth.

Hers no such low-hung fortunes.   Thus to stand

Supreme one instant at that dizzy height,

With no hoarse raven croaking in her ear

The certain doom, and then to have life's rose

Struck swiftly from the cheek, and so escape

Love's death, black treason, friend's ingratitude,

The pang of separation, chill of age,

The grief that in an empty cradle lies,

And all the unspoke sorrow women know —

That was, in truth, to have a happy reign !

Has thine been happier, Sovereign of the Sea,

In that long-mateless pilgrimage to death?

Or thine, whose beauty like a star illumed

Awhile the dark and angry sky of France,

Thy kingdom shrunken to two exiled graves?

Sweet old-world maid, a gentler fate was yours !

Would he had wed your story to his verse

Who from the misty land of legend brought

Helen of Troy to gladden English eyes.

There 's many a queen that lived her grandeur out,

Gray-haired and broken, might have envied you,

Your Majesty, that reigned a single day !

All this, as 't were between two beats of heart,

Flashed through my mind, so lightning-like is
> thought.

With lifted eyes expectant, there she sat

Whose words had sent my fancy over-sea,

Her lip still trembling with its own soft speech,

As for a moment trembles the curved spray

Whence some winged melody has taken flight.

How every circumstance of time and place

Upon the glass of memory lives again ! —

The bleak New England road ; the level boughs

Like bars of iron across the setting sun ;

The gray ribbed clouds piled up against the West ;

The windows splashed with frost ; the fire-lit
room,

And in the antique chair that slight girl-shape,

The auburn braid about the saintly brows

Making a nimbus, and she white as snow !

"Dear Heart," I said, "the humblest place is
best

For gentle souls — the throne's foot, not the
throne.

The storms that smite the dizzy solitudes

Where monarchs sit — most lonely folk are
they ! —

Oft leave the vale unscathed; there dwells

content,

If so content have habitation here.

Never have I in annals read or rhyme

Of queen save one that found not at the end

The cup too bitter ; never queen save one,

And she — her empire lasted but a day !

Yet that brief breath of time did she so fill

With mercy, love, and holy charity

As more rich made it than long-drawn-out years

Of such weed-life as drinks the lavish sun

And rots unflower'd."   " Straight tell me of that

queen ! "

Cried Edith ; " Brunhild, in my legend here,

Is lovely — was that other still more fair ?

And had she not a Siegfried at the court

To steal her talisman ? — that Siegfried did

At Günther's bidding.   Was your queen not

 loved ?

Tell me it all ! "   With chin upon her palm

Resting, she listened, and within her eyes

The sapphire deepened as I told the tale

Of the girl-empress in the dawn of Time —

A flower that on the vermeil brink of May

Died, with its folded whiteness for a shroud ;

A strain of music that, ere it was mixed

With baser voices, floated up to heaven.

 Without was silence, for the wind was spent

That all the day had pleaded at the door.

Against the crimson sunset elm and oak

Stood black and motionless ; among the boughs

The sad wind slumbered.   Silence filled the

 room,

Save when from out the crumbled apple branch

Came the wren's twitter, faint, and fainter now,

Like a bird's note far heard in twilight woods.

No other sound was.   Presently a hand

Stole into mine, and rested there, inert,

Like some new-gathered snowy hyacinth,

So white and cold and delicate it was.

I know not what dark shadow crossed my heart,

What vague presentiment, but as I stooped

To lift the slender fingers to my lip,

I saw it through a mist of strangest tears —

The   thin   white   hand   invisible   Death   had
            touched !

INTERLUDES

INSOMNIA

SLUMBER, hasten down this way,
    And, ere midnight dies,
Silence lay upon my lips,
    Darkness on my eyes.

Send me a fantastic dream;
    Fashion me afresh;
Into some celestial thing
    Change this mortal flesh.

Well I know one may not choose;
    One is helpless still

In the purple realm of Sleep :

　　Use me as you will.

Let me be a frozen pine

　　In dead glacier lands ;

Let me pant, a leopard stretched

　　On the Libyan sands.

Silver fin or scarlet wing

　　Grant me, either one ;

Sink me deep in emerald glooms,

　　Lift me to the sun.

Or of me a gargoyle make,

　　Face of ape or gnome,

Such as frights the tavern-boor

　　Reeling drunken home.

Work on me your own caprice,

    Give me any shape ;

Only, Slumber, from myself

    Let myself escape !

SEEMING DEFEAT

THE woodland silence, one time stirred

By the soft pathos of some passing bird,

Is not the same it was before.

The spot where once, unseen, a flower

Has held its fragile chalice to the shower,

Is different for evermore.

Unheard, unseen,

A spell has been !

O thou that breathest year by year

Music that falls unheeded on the ear,

Take heart, fate has not baffled thee !

Thou that with tints of earth and skies

Fillest thy canvas for unseeing eyes,

Thou hast not labored futilely.

Unheard, unseen,

A spell has been !

TWO MOODS

I

BETWEEN the budding and the falling leaf

Stretch happy skies ;

With colors and sweet cries

Of mating birds in uplands and in glades

The world is rife.

Then on a sudden all the music dies,

The color fades.

How fugitive and brief

Is mortal life

Between the budding and the falling leaf !

O short-breathed music, dying on the tongue

Ere half the mystic canticle be sung !

O harp of life, so speedily unstrung !

Who, if 't were his to choose, would know again

The bitter sweetness of the lost refrain,

Its rapture, and its pain ?

II

Though I be shut in darkness, and become

Insentient dust blown idly here and there,

I count oblivion a scant price to pay

For having once had held against my lip

Life's brimming cup of hydromel and rue —

For having once known woman's holy love

And a child's kiss, and for a little space

Been boon companion to the Day and Night,

Fed on the odors of the summer dawn,

And folded in the beauty of the stars.

Dear Lord, though I be changed to senseless clay,

And serve the potter as he turns his wheel,

I thank Thee for the gracious gift of tears !

A PARABLE

ONE went East, and one went West

    Across the wild sea-foam,

And both were on the self-same quest.

Now one there was who cared for naught,

    So stayed at home :

Yet of the three 't was only he

Who reached the goal — by him unsought.

"GREAT CAPTAIN, GLORIOUS IN OUR WARS"

GREAT Captain, glorious in our wars —

No meed of praise we hold from him ;

About his brow we wreathe the stars

The coming ages shall not dim.

The cloud-sent man !   Was it not he

That from the hand of adverse fate

Snatched the white flower of victory ?

He spoke no word, but saved the State.

Yet History, as she brooding bends

Above the tablet on her knee,

The impartial stylus half suspends,

And fain would blot the cold decree :

"The iron hand and sleepless care

That stayed disaster scarce availed

To serve him when he came to wear

The civic laurel : there he failed."

Who runs may read ; but nothing mars

That nobler record, unforgot.

Great Captain, glorious in our wars —

All else the heart remembers not.

A REFRAIN

HIGH in a tower she sings,

I, passing by beneath,

Pause and listen, and catch

These words of passionate breath —

" *Asphodel, flower of Life; amaranth, flower of*

Death ! "

Sweet voice, sweet unto tears !

What is this that she saith ?

Poignant, mystical — hark !

Again, with passionate breath —

" *Asphodel, flower of Life; amaranth, flower of*

Death ! "

" A CRAFTY Persian set this stone;

    A dusk Sultana wore it;

  And from her slender finger, sir,

    A ruthless Arab tore it.

" A ruby, like a drop of blood —

    That deep-in tint that lingers

  And seems to melt, perchance was caught

    From those poor mangled fingers !

" A spendthrift got it from the knave,

    And tost it, like a blossom,

That night into a dancing-girl's

Accurst and balmy bosom.

"And so it went.   One day a Jew

At Cairo chanced to spy it

Amid a one-eyed peddler's pack,

And did not care to buy it —

"Yet bought it all the same.   You see,

The Jew he knew a jewel.

He bought it cheap to sell it dear :

The ways of trade are cruel.

"But I — be Allah's all the praise ! —

Such avarice, I scoff it !

If I buy cheap, why, I sell cheap,

Content with modest profit.

" This ring — such chasing! look, milord,

    What workmanship!   By Heaven,

  The price I name you makes the thing

    As if the thing were given!

" A stone without a flaw!   A queen

    Might not disdain to wear it.

  Three hundred roubles buys the stone ;

    No kopeck less, I swear it ! "

Thus Hassan, holding up the ring

    To me, no eager buyer. —

  A hundred roubles was not much

    To pay so sweet a liar !

THE WINTER ROBIN

Sursum corda

Now is that sad time of year

When no flower or leaf is here;

When in misty Southern ways

Oriole and jay have flown,

And of all sweet birds, alone

The robin stays.

So give thanks at Christmas-tide:

Hopes of spring-time yet abide!

See, in spite of darksome days,

Wind and rain and bitter chill,

Snow, and sleet-hung branches, still

The robin stays!

THE SAILING OF THE AUTOCRAT

ON BOARD THE S. S. CEPHALONIA, APRIL 26,
1886

I

O WIND and Wave, be kind to him!

So, Wave and Wind, we give thee thanks!

O Fog, that from Newfoundland Banks

Makest the blue bright ocean dim,

Delay him not! And ye who snare

The wayworn shipman with your song,

Go pipe your ditties otherwhere

While this brave vessel plows along!

If still to lure him be your thought,

O phantoms of the watery zone,

Look lively lest yourselves get caught

With music sweeter than your own !

II

Yet, soft sea-spirits, be not mute ;

Murmur about the prow, and make

Melodious the west-wind's lute.

For him may radiant mornings break

From out the bosom of the deep,

And golden noons above him bend,

And fortunate constellations keep

Bright vigils to his journey's end !

III

Take him, green Erin, to thy breast !

Keep him, gray London — for a while !

In him we send thee of our best,

Our wisest word, our blithest smile —

Our epigram, alert and pat,

That kills with joy the folly hit —

Our Yankee Tsar, our Autocrat

Of all the happy realms of wit !

Take him and keep him — but forbear

To keep him more than half a year. . . .

His presence will be sunshine there,

His absence will be shadow here !

CRADLE SONG

I

ERE the moon begins to rise

Or a star to shine,

All the bluebells close their eyes —

So close thine,

Thine, dear, thine !

II

Birds are sleeping in the nest

On the swaying bough,

Thus, against the mother-breast —

So sleep thou,

Sleep, sleep, sleep !

BROKEN MUSIC

A note

All out of tune in this world's instrument.

AMY LEVY.

I KNOW not in what fashion she was made,

    Nor what her voice was, when she used to

        speak,

Nor if the silken lashes threw a shade

        On wan or rosy cheek.

I picture her with sorrowful vague eyes

    Illumed with such strange gleams of inner light

As linger in the drift of London skies

        Ere twilight turns to night.

I know not ; I conjecture.   'T was a girl
  That with her own most gentle desperate hand
From out God's mystic setting plucked life's
    pearl —
      'T is hard to understand.

So precious life is !   Even to the old
  The hours are as a miser's coins, and she —
Within her hands lay youth's unminted gold
      And all felicity.

The winged impetuous spirit, the white flame
  That was her soul once, whither has it flown ?
Above her brow gray lichens blot her name
      Upon the carven stone.

This is her Book of Verses — wren-like notes,
  Shy franknesses, blind gropings, haunting fears ;

At times across the chords abruptly floats

    A mist of passionate tears.

A fragile lyre too tensely keyed and strung,

    A broken music, weirdly incomplete :

Here a proud mind, self-baffled and self-stung,

    Lies coiled in dark defeat.

ART

" LET art be all in all," one time I said,

And straightway stirred the hypercritic gall:

I said not, "Let technique be all in all,"

But art — a wider meaning. Worthless, dead —

The shell without its pearl, the corpse of things —

Mere words are, till the spirit lend them wings.

The poet who wakes no soul within his lute

Falls short of art: 't were better he were mute.

The workmanship wherewith the gold is wrought

Adds yet a richness to the richest gold:

Who lacks the art to shape his thought, I hold,

Were little poorer if he lacked the thought.

The statue's slumber were unbroken still

In the dull marble, had the hand no skill.

Disparage not the magic touch that gives

The formless thought the grace whereby it lives !

"WHEN FROM THE TENSE CHORDS OF THAT MIGHTY LYRE"

JANUARY, 1892

I

WHEN from the tense chords of that mighty lyre

The Master's hand, relaxing, falls away,

   And those rich strings are silent for all time,

Then shall Love pine, and Passion lack her fire,

   And Faith seem voiceless.   Man to man shall

say,

   "Dead is the last of England's Lords of

Rhyme."

II

Yet — stay! there's one, a later laureled brow,

With purple blood of poets in his veins ;

Him has the Muse claimed ; him might Mar-

lowe own ;

Greek Sappho's son ! — men's praises seek him

now.

Happy the realm where one such voice re-

mains !

His the dropt wreath and the unenvied

throne.

III

The wreath the world gives, not the mimic wreath

That chance might make the gift of king or

queen.

O finder of undreamed-of harmonies !

Since Shelley's lips were hushed by cruel death,

What lyric voice so sweet as this has been

Borne to us on the winds from over seas ?

A SERENADE

Imp of Dreams, when she 's asleep,

To her snowy chamber creep,

And straight whisper in her ear

What, awake, she will not hear —

Imp of Dreams, when she 's asleep.

Tell her, so she may repent,

That no rose withholds its scent,

That no bird that has a song

Hoards the music summer-long —

Tell her, so she may repent.

Tell her there 's naught else to do,

If to-morrow's skies be blue,

But to come, with civil speech,

And walk with me to Chelsea Beach —

    Tell her there 's naught else to do !

      Tell her, so she may repent —

        Imp of Dreams, when she 's asleep !

A BRIDAL MEASURE

FOR S. F.

GIFTS they sent her manifold,

Diamonds and pearls and gold.

One there was among the throng

Had not Midas' touch at need :

He against a sylvan reed

Set his lips and breathed a song.

Bid bright Flora, as she comes,

Snatch a spray of orange blooms

For a maiden's hair.

Let the Hours their aprons fill

With mignonette and daffodil,

 And all that 's fair.

For her bosom fetch the rose

 That is rarest —

Not that either these or those

 Could by any happening be

 Ornaments to such as she ;

They 'll but show, when she is dressed,

 She is fairer than the fairest

And out-betters what is best !

IMOGEN

LEONATUS POSTHUMUS *speaks:*

SORROW, make a verse for me

That shall breathe all human grieving ;

Let it be love's exequy,

. And the knell of all believing !

Let it such sweet pathos have

As a violet on a grave,

Or a dove's moan when his mate

Leaves the new nest desolate.

Sorrow, Sorrow, by this token,

Braid a wreath for Beauty's head. . . .

Valley-lilies, one or two,

Should be woven with the rue.

Sorrow, Sorrow, all is spoken —

She is dead !

SEVEN SONNETS

I

OUTWARD BOUND

I LEAVE behind me the elm-shadowed square

And carven portals of the silent street,

And wander on with listless, vagrant feet

Through seaward-leading alleys, till the air

Smells of the sea, and straightway then the care

Slips from my heart, and life once more is sweet.

At the lane's ending lie the white-winged fleet.

O restless Fancy, whither wouldst thou fare?

Here are brave pinions that shall take thee far —

Gaunt hulks of Norway; ships of red Ceylon;

Slim-masted lovers of the blue Azores !

'T is but an instant hence to Zanzibar,

Or to the regions of the Midnight Sun :

Ionian isles are thine, and all the fairy shores !

II

ELLEN TERRY IN "THE MERCHANT OF VENICE"

As there she lives and moves upon the scene,

So lived and moved this radiant womanhood

In Shakespeare's vision; in such wise she
  stood

Smiling upon Bassanio; such her mien

When pity dimmed her eyelids' golden sheen,

Hearing Antonio's story, and the blood

Paled on her cheek, and all her lightsome mood

Was gone. This shape in Shakespeare's
  thought has been !

Thus dreamt he of her in gray London town ;

Such were her eyes ; on such gold-colored hair

The grave young judge's velvet cap was set ;

So stood she lovely in her crimson gown.

Mine were a happy cast, could I but snare

Her beauty in a sonnet's fragile net !

III

THE POETS

When this young Land has reached its wrinkled
    prime,

And we are gone and all our songs are done,

And naught is left unchanged beneath the sun,

What other singers shall the womb of Time

Bring forth to reap the sunny slopes of rhyme?

For surely till the thread of life be spun

The world shall not lack poets, though but one

Make lonely music like a vesper chime

Above the heedless turmoil of the street.

What new strange voices shall be given to these,

What richer accents of melodious breath ?

Yet shall they, baffled, lie at Nature's feet

Searching the volume of her mysteries,

And vainly question the fixed eyes of Death.

IV

THE UNDISCOVERED COUNTRY .

FOREVER am I conscious, moving here,

That should I step a little space aside

I pass the boundary of some glorified

Invisible domain — it lies so near!

Yet nothing know we of that dim frontier

Which each must cross, whatever fate betide,

To reach the heavenly cities where abide

(Thus Sorrow whispers) those that were most
     dear,

Now all transfigured in celestial light!

Shall we indeed behold them, thine and mine,

Whose going hence made black the noonday

sun ? —

Strange is it that across the narrow night

They fling us not some token, or make sign

That all beyond is not Oblivion.

V

BOOKS AND SEASONS

BECAUSE the sky is blue ; because blithe May

Masks in the wren's note and the lilac's hue ;

Because — in fine, because the sky is blue

I will read none but piteous tales to-day.

Keep happy laughter till the skies be gray,

And the sad season cypress wears, and rue ;

Then, when the wind is moaning in the flue,

And ways are dark, bid Chaucer make us gay.

But now a little sadness ! All too sweet

This springtide riot, this most poignant air,

This sensuous sphere of color and perfume !

So listen, love, while I the woes repeat

Of Hamlet and Ophelia, and that pair

Whose bridal bed was builded in a tomb.

VI

REMINISCENCE

THOUGH I am native to this frozen zone

That half the twelvemonth torpid lies, or dead ;

Though the cold azure arching overhead

And the Atlantic's never-ending moan

Are mine by heritage, I must have known

Life otherwhere in epochs long since fled ;

For in my veins some Orient blood is red,

And through my thought are lotus blossoms

    blown.

I do remember . . . it was just at dusk,

Near a walled garden at the river's turn

(A thousand summers seem but yesterday !),

A Nubian girl, more sweet than Khoorja musk,

Came to the water-tank to fill her urn,

And, with the urn, she bore my heart away!

VII

ANDROMEDA

THE smooth-worn coin and threadbare classic
phrase

Of Grecian myths that did beguile my youth,

Beguile me not as in the olden days :

I think more grief and beauty dwell with truth.

Andromeda, in fetters by the sea,

Star-pale with anguish till young Perseus came,

Less moves me with her suffering than she,

The slim girl figure fettered to dark shame,

That nightly haunts the park, there, like a shade,

Trailing her wretchedness from street to street.

See where she passes — neither wife nor maid.

How all mere fiction crumbles at her feet!

Here is woe's self, and not the mask of woe:

A legend's shadow shall not move you so!

NOURMADEE

NOURMADEE

O HASSEM, greeting ! Peace be thine !

With thee and thine be all things well !

Give refuge to these words of mine.

The strange mischance which late befell

Thy servant must have reached thine ear ;

Rumor has flung it far and wide,

With dark additions, as I hear.

When They-Say speaks, what ills betide !

So lend no credence, O my Friend,

To scandals, fattening as they fly.

Love signs and seals the roll I send :

Read thou the truth with lenient eye.

In Yússuf's garden at Tangier

This happened.   In his cool kiosk

We sat partaking of his cheer —

Thou know'st that garden by the Mosque

Of Irma; stately palms are there,

And silver fish in marble tanks,

And scents of jasmine in the air —

We sat and feasted, with due thanks

To Allah, till the pipes were brought;

And no one spoke, for Pleasure laid

Her finger on the lips of Thought.

Then, on a sudden, came a maid,

With tambourine, to dance for us —

Allah il' Allah ! it was she,

The slave-girl from the Bosphorus
That Yússuf purchased recently.

Long narrow eyes, as black as black !
And melting, like the stars in June ;
Tresses of night drawn smoothly back
From eyebrows like the crescent moon.
She paused an instant with bowed head,
Then, at a motion of her wrist,
A veil of gossamer outspread
And wrapt her in a silver mist.
Her tunic was of Tiflis green
Shot through with many a starry speck ;
The zone that claspt it might have been
A collar for a cygnet's neck.
None of the twenty charms she lacked
Demanded for perfection's grace ;

Charm upon charm in her was packed

Like rose leaves in a costly vase.

Full in the lanterns' colored light

She seemed a thing of Paradise.

I knew not if I saw aright,

Or if my vision told me lies.

Those lanterns spread a cheating glare ;

Such stains they threw from bough and vine

As if the slave-boys, here and there,

Had spilt a jar of brilliant wine.

And then the fountain's drowsy fall,

The burning aloes' heavy scent,

The night, the place, the hour — they all

Were full of subtle blandishment.

Much had I heard of Nourmadee —

The name of this fair slenderness —

Whom Yússuf kept with lock and key

Because her beauty wrought distress

In all men's hearts that gazed on it ;

And much I marveled why, this night,

Yússuf should have the little wit

To lift her veil for our delight.

For though the other guests were old —

Grave, worthy merchants, three from Fez

(These mostly dealt in dyes and gold),

Cloth merchants two, from Mekīnez —

Though they were old and gray and dry,

Forgetful of their youth's desires,

My case was different, for I

Still knew the touch of springtime fires.

And straightway as I looked on her

I bit my lip, grew ill at ease,

And in my veins was that strange stir

Which clothes with bloom the almond-trees.

O Shape of blended fire and snow !

Each clime to her some spell had lent —

The North her cold, the South her glow,

Her languors all the Orient.

Her scarf was as the cloudy fleece

The moon draws round its loveliness,

That so its beauty may increase

The more in being seen the less.

And as she moved, and seemed to float —

So floats a swan ! — in sweet unrest,

A string of sequins at her throat

Went clink and clink against her breast.

And what did some birth-fairy do

But set a mole, a golden dot,

Close to her lip — to pierce men through !

How could I look and love her not ?

Yet heavy was my heart as stone,

For well I knew that love was vain ;

To love the thing one may not own ! —

I saw how all my peace was slain.

Coffers of ingots Yússuf had,

Houses on land, and ships at sea,

And I — alas ! was I gone mad,

To cast my eyes on Nourmadee !

I strove to thrust her from my mind,

I bent my brows, and turned away,

And wished that Fate had struck me blind

Ere I had come to know that day.

I fixed my thoughts on this and that ;

Assessed the worth of Yússuf's ring ;

Counted the colors in the mat —

And then a bird began to sing,

A bulbul hidden in a bough.

From time to time it loosed a strain

Of moonlit magic that, somehow,

Brought comfort to my troubled brain.

But when the girl once, creeping close,

Half stooped, and looked me in the face,

My reason fled, and I arose

And cried to Yússuf, from my place :

" O Yússuf, give to me this girl !

You are so rich and I so poor !

You would not miss one little pearl

Like that from out your countless store ! "

" ' This girl ' ?   What girl ?   No girl is here ! "

Cried Yússuf with his eyes agleam ;

" Now, by the Prophet, it is clear

Our friend has had a pleasant dream ! "

(And then it seems that I awoke,

And stared around, no little dazed

At finding naught of what I spoke :

The guests sat silent and amazed.)

Then Yússuf — of all mortal men

This Yússuf has a mocking tongue ! —

Stood at my side, and spoke again :

"O Mirtzy, I too once was young.

With mandolin or dulcimer

I 've waited many a midnight through,

Content to catch one glimpse of Her,

And have my turban drenched with dew.

By Her I mean some slim Malay,

Some Andalusian with her fan

(For I have traveled in my day),

Or some swart beauty of Soudan.

No Barmecide was I to fare

On fancy's shadowy wine and meat;

No phantom moulded out of air

Had spells to lure me to her feet.

O Mirtzy, be it understood

I blame you not.   Your sin is slight! —

You fled the world of flesh and blood,

And loved a vision of the night!

Sweeter than musk such visions be

As come to poets when they sleep !

You dreamed you saw fair Nourmadee ?

Go to ! it is a pearl I keep ! "

By Allah, but his touch was true !

And I was humbled to the dust

That I in those grave merchants' view

Should seem a thing no man might trust.

For he of creeping things is least

Who, while he breaks of friendship's bread,

Betrays the giver of the feast.

"Good friends, I 'm not that man!" I said.

"O Yússuf, shut not Pardon's gate!

The words I spake I no wise meant.

Who holds the threads of Time and Fate

Sends dreams. I dreamt the dream he sent.

I am as one that from a trance

Awakes confused, and reasons ill;

The world of men invites his glance,

The world of shadows claims him still.

I see those lights among the leaves,

Yourselves I see, sedate and wise,

And yet some finer sense perceives

A presence that eludes the eyes.

Of what is gone there seems to stay

Some subtlety, to mock my pains:

So, when a rose is borne away,

The fragrance of the rose remains!"

Then Yússuf laughed, Abdallah leered,

And Melik coughed behind his hand,

And lean Ben-Auda stroked his beard

As who should say, "We understand!"

And though the fault was none of mine,

As I explained and made appear,

Since then I 've not been asked to dine

In Yússuf's garden at Tangier.

Farewell, O Hassem!   Peace be thine!

With thee and thine be always Peace!

To virtue let thy steps incline,

And may thy shadow not decrease!

Get wealth — wealth makes the dullard's jest

Seem witty where true wit falls flat;

Do good, for goodness still is best —

But then the Koran tells thee that.

Know Patience here, and later Bliss;

Grow wise, trust woman, doubt not man;

And when thou dinest out — mark this —

Beware of wines from Ispahan!

FOOTNOTES

FIREFLIES

SEE where at intervals the firefly's spark

Glimmers, and melts into the fragrant dark ;

Gilds a leaf's edge one happy instant, then

Leaves darkness all a mystery again !

PROBLEM

So closely knit are mind and brain,

Such web and woof are soul and clay,

How is it, being rent in twain,

One part shall live, and one decay ?

ORIGINALITY

No bird has ever uttered note

That was not in some first bird's throat ;

Since Eden's freshness and man's fall

No rose has been original.

KISMET

A GLANCE, a word — and joy or pain

Befalls ; what was no more shall be.

How slight the links are in the chain

That binds us to our destiny !

A HINT FROM HERRICK

No slightest golden rhyme he wrote

That held not something men must quote ;

Thus by design or chance did he

Drop anchors to posterity.

PESSIMISTIC POETS

I LITTLE read those poets who have made

A noble art a pessimistic trade,

And trained their Pegasus to draw a hearse

Through endless avenues of drooping verse.

HOSPITALITY

WHEN friends are at your hearthside met,

Sweet courtesy has done its most

If you have made each guest forget

That he himself is not the host.

POINTS OF VIEW

BONNET in hand, obsequious and discreet,

The butcher that served Shakespeare with his

    meat

Doubtless esteemed him little, as a man

Who knew not how the market prices ran.

THE TWO MASKS

I GAVE my heart its freedom to be gay

Or grave at will, when life was in its May ;

So I have gone, a pilgrim through the years,

With more of laughter in my scrip than tears.

QUITS

IF my best wines mislike thy taste,

And my best service win thy frown,

Then tarry not, I bid thee haste ;

There 's many another Inn in town.

www.ingramcontent.com/pod-product-compliance
Lightning Source LLC
Chambersburg PA
CBHW020801020726
47495CB00008B/2533